Five reasons why we t[...] you'll love this book!

Winnie AND Wilbur
THE NEW COMPUTER

Even Winnie's postman is magic!

You'll discover what Winnie and Wilbur have for breakfast.

There is so much to spot in every picture.

You can join in when Winnie shouts 'Abracadabra!'

You can take the Winnie and Wilbur challenge: how many mice (not including the computer mouse!) can you find?

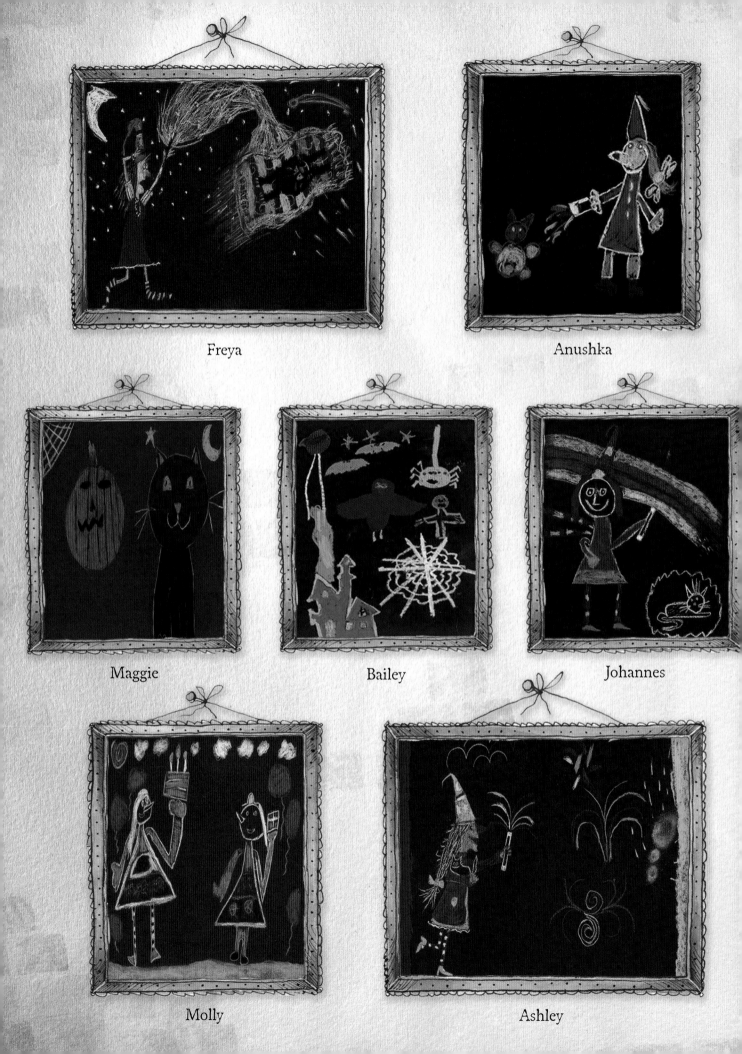

Freya

Anushka

Maggie

Bailey

Johannes

Molly

Ashley

Amber

Jun-Yeong

Pablo

Matilda

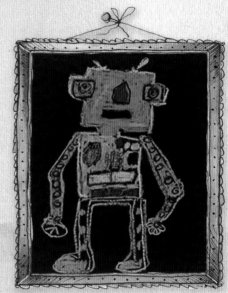

Marwin

Hasan

Rebecca

Thank you to all these schools for helping with the endpapers:

St Barnabas Primary School, Oxford; St Ebbe's Primary School, Oxford; Marcham Primary School, Abingdon; St Michael's C.E. Aided Primary School, Oxford; St Bede's RC Primary School, Jarrow; The Western Academy, Beijing, China; John King School, Pinxton; Neston Primary School, Neston; Star of the Sea RC Primary School, Whitley Bay; José Jorge Letria Primary School, Cascais, Portugal; Dunmore Primary School, Abingdon; Özel Bahçeşehir İlköğretim Okulu, Istanbul, Turkey; the International School of Amsterdam, the Netherlands; Princethorpe Infant School, Birmingham.

To my lovely sister Moya and her
beautiful husband Basil—V.T.

To Katya Wright—K.P.

OXFORD
UNIVERSITY PRESS

Great Clarendon Street, Oxford OX2 6DP

Oxford University Press is a department of the University of Oxford. It furthers the University's objective of excellence in research, scholarship,and education by publishing worldwide. Oxford is a registered trade mark of Oxford University Press in the UK and in certain other countries

Text copyright © Valerie Thomas 2003
Illustrations copyright © Korky Paul 2003, 2016
The moral rights of the author and artist
have been asserted

Database right Oxford University Press (maker)

First published as *Winnie's New Computer* in 2003
This edition first published in 2016

British Library Cataloguing in Publication Data available

ISBN: 978-0-19-274826-3 (paperback)
ISBN: 978-0-19-274916-1 (paperback and CD)

10 9 8 7 6 5 4 3 2 1

Printed in China

Paper used in the production of this book is a natural, recyclable product made from wood grown in sustainable forests. The manufacturing process conforms to the environmental regulations of the country of origin

www.winnieandwilbur.com

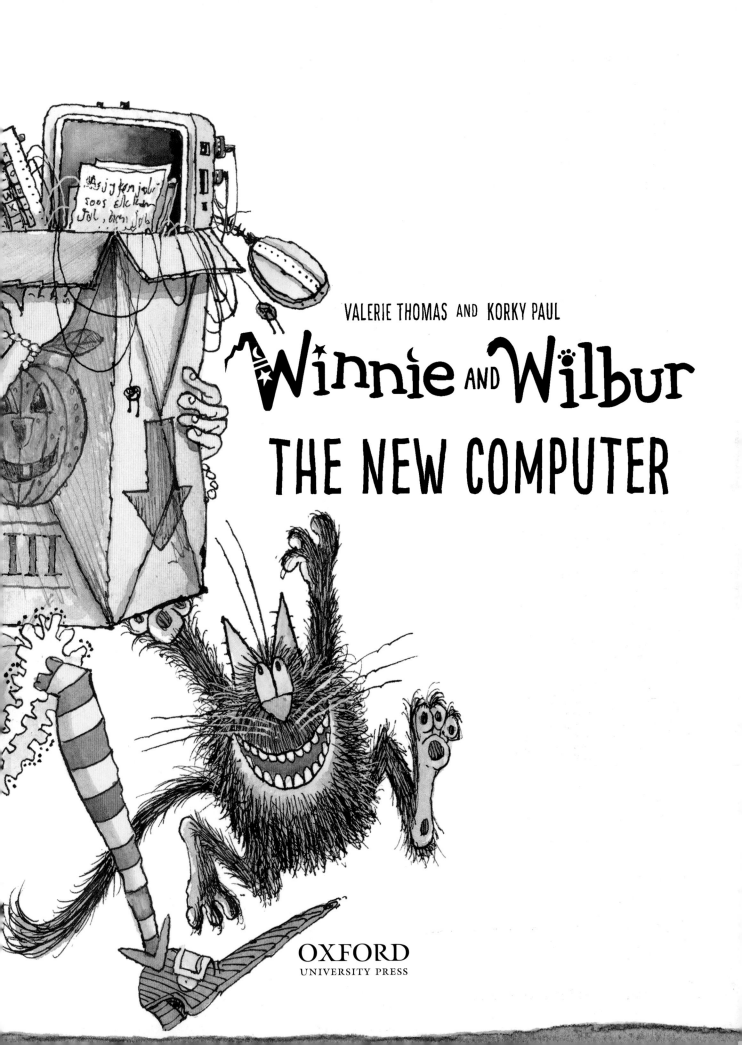

VALERIE THOMAS AND KORKY PAUL

Winnie and Wilbur
THE NEW COMPUTER

OXFORD

UNIVERSITY PRESS

Winnie the Witch had a new computer. She was very excited. Her cat, Wilbur, was excited too. He thought something interesting might happen and he didn't want to miss it.

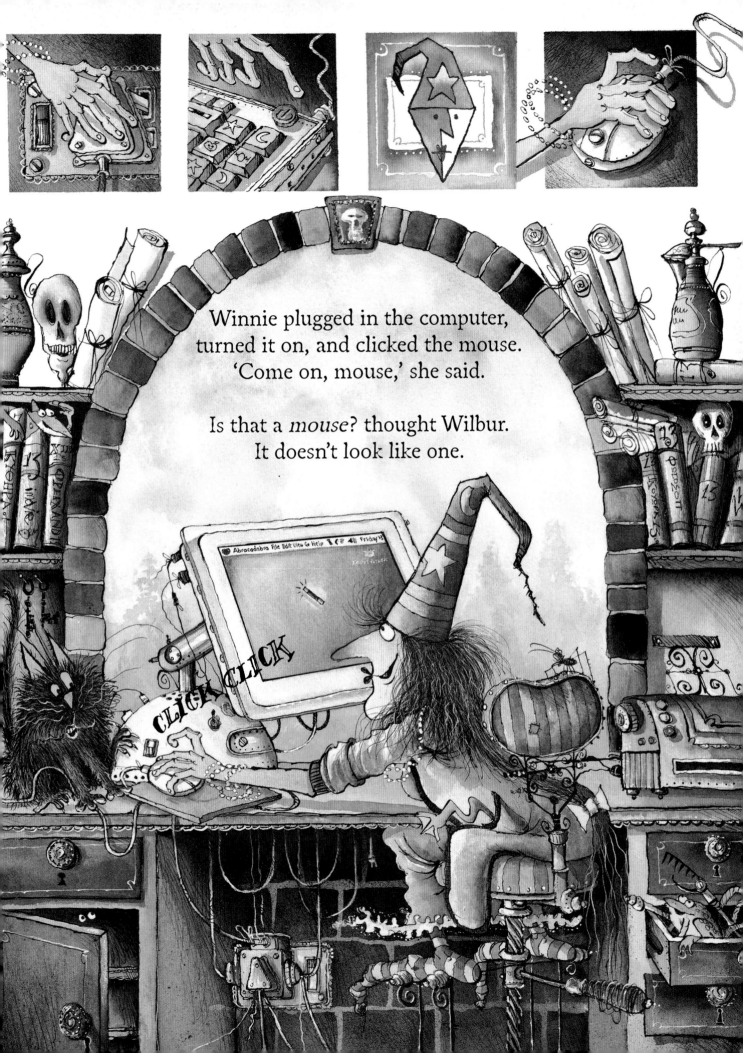

Winnie plugged in the computer,
turned it on, and clicked the mouse.
'Come on, mouse,' she said.

Is that a *mouse*? thought Wilbur.
It doesn't look like one.

Winnie went on to the internet.
Wilbur wanted a closer look at the mouse.
He patted it.

'Don't touch the mouse, Wilbur!' said Winnie.
'I want to order a new wand!'

Wilbur patted the mouse again. **Pat, pat.**

Winnie was cross.
She put Wilbur outside.
She didn't notice
that it was raining . . .

Wilbur noticed it was raining. He was getting
wet. He watched Winnie through the window.
She was having a good time.

She ordered her new wand, and then
she visited some websites for witches.
They had some very funny jokes.
'Ha, ha, ha,' laughed Winnie.

Wilbur *wasn't* laughing.
The rain was dripping off his whiskers.
'Meeow,' he cried. 'Meeeoooww!'
But Winnie didn't hear him.

That mouse has put a spell on her, thought Wilbur.

plop plop plop
plop plop Plop plop plop
plop Plop

Plop, plop, plop.
'What's that noise?'
asked Winnie.

It was the rain.
It was coming through the roof.

'Oh no!' said Winnie. 'The rain
will ruin my new computer!
I need the Roof Repair Spell.'

But she couldn't find her Book of Spells
or her magic wand anywhere.

'Oh, where are they?' she cried
as the rain plopped down.

At last she found them.
She waved her wand seven
times at the roof, and shouted,

'Abracadabra!'

The roof stopped leaking.
'Thank goodness,' Winnie said.

Then she had a wonderful idea.

'If I scan all my spells into the computer,' she said,
'I won't need my Book of Spells any more.
I won't need to wave my magic wand.
I'll just use the computer. One click will do the trick.'

So Winnie loaded all her spells into the new computer.
'I'd better try it out,' she said. 'What shall I do?'

'I know, I'll turn Wilbur into a blue cat.'

She let Wilbur inside. She went to
the computer, clicked the mouse,
and Wilbur was bright blue.

'Good!' said Winnie.
'It works!'

CLICK

CLICK

She clicked the mouse, and Wilbur was a black cat again.
An angry, wet, black cat.

'Well, Wilbur,' said Winnie, 'I won't need my Book of Spells or my magic wand any more.'

And she put them out for the dustman to take away.

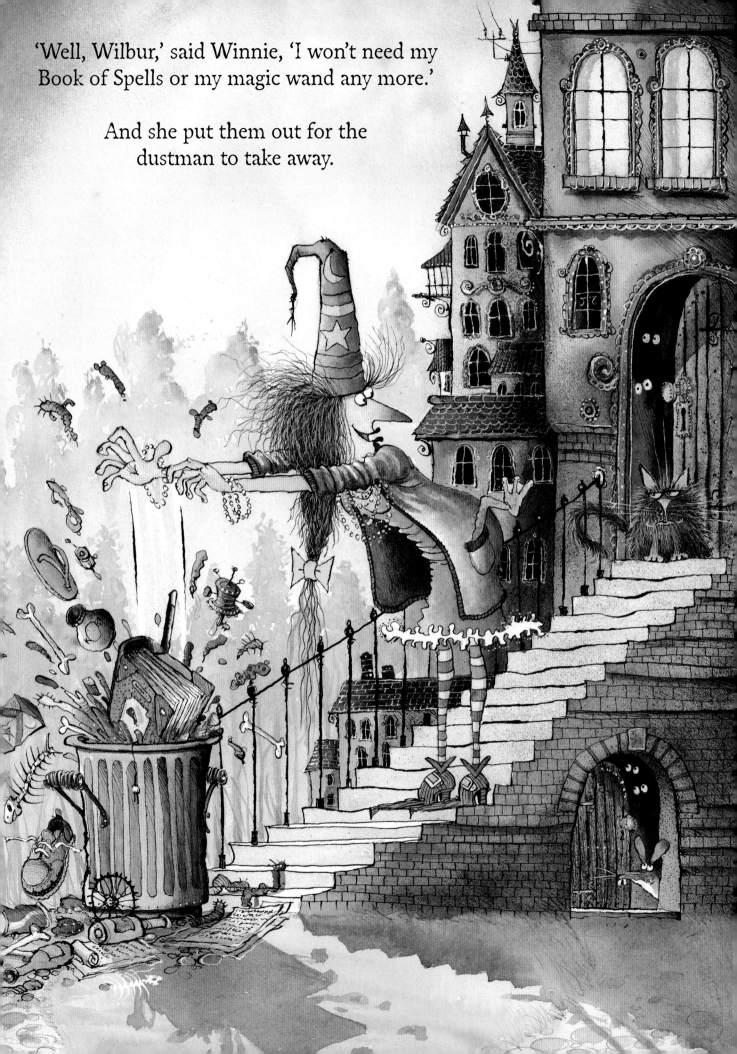

That night, Wilbur waited until
he could hear Winnie snoring.
Then he crept downstairs.

He was going to see about that mouse.

He patted it.
Nothing happened.
'Meeow, grrrrssss!' he snarled.
He grabbed the mouse, tossed it
into the air, and rolled onto his back.

Winnie had a lovely sleep.
In the morning she came downstairs
for her breakfast.

'Breakfast, Wilbur,' she called.
'Where are you, Wilbur?'

She looked in the garden, in the bathroom, in all the cupboards.
No Wilbur. Then she looked in the computer room . . .

'OH NO!!!' cried Winnie.
'Wilbur, where are you? And where's the computer?'

She reached into the cupboard for her Book of Spells. She put her hand in her pocket for her magic wand.

Then she remembered.

She ran to the window. The dustman was tipping her rubbish into his truck.

'Stop!' shouted Winnie. 'STOP!' But it was too late. The dustman couldn't hear her. He jumped into his truck and drove away.

'What shall I do?' cried Winnie.

Then another truck came through the gate.
'My new wand!' said Winnie.
'It's arrived! Thank goodness!'

She grabbed the new wand, waved it once, and shouted,

'Abracadabra!'

The Book of Spells flew out of the
rubbish truck, up into the air . . .

. . . and dropped into her arms.

Winnie rushed inside, and looked up the spell to make things come back.
Then she shut her eyes, waved her wand four times, and shouted,

'Abracadabra!'

The computer and Wilbur came back.
'Oh, Wilbur!' said Winnie. 'You're bright blue!
Whatever happened?
Never mind, I'll change you back to black again.'

She went to the computer
and clicked the mouse.
Wilbur was a black cat again.

'Good,' said Winnie.
'It still works. But I think I'll keep my
Book of Spells and my magic wand.
I might need them one day.'

Bethany

Katia

Eun-Jae

Kathleen

Ji-Eun

Jenny

Sara

Fraser

Ka Keung

Selin

Selin

Olivia

Siyabend

Kieran

A note for grown-ups

Oxford Owl is a FREE and easy-to-use website packed with support and advice about everything to do with reading.

Informative videos

Hints, tips and fun activities

Top tips from top writers for reading with your child

Help with choosing picture books

For this expert advice and much, much more about how children learn to read and how to keep them reading ...

LOOK
for Oxford Owl
www.oxfordowl.co.uk